Chicken Little

Retold by M. J. York

Illustrated by Teri Weidner

The Child's World®
1980 Lookout Drive · Mankato, MN 56003-1705
800-599-READ · www.childsworld.com

Acknowledgments
The Child's World®: Mary Berendes, Publishing Director
The Design Lab: Kathleen Petelinsek, Design
Red Line Editorial: Editorial direction

ISBN 9781614732136
LCCN 2012932695

Printed in the United States of America
Mankato, MN
July 2012
PA02125

Chicken Little woke up one beautiful fall morning. The leaves were falling down, red, orange, yellow, and brown. She went for a walk under the tall oak trees.

An acorn fell from a tall oak tree. It hit Chicken Little on the head with a PLUNK!

"The sky is falling, the sky is falling!" she yelled. "I must run and warn the king!"

She ran and ran through the red, orange, yellow, and brown leaves. She ran and ran past the tall oak trees. She ran into Henny Penny.

"Chicken Little, what's wrong?" asked Henny Penny.

"The sky is falling, the sky is falling! We must run and warn the king!" cried Chicken Little.

"How do you know the sky is falling?" asked Henny Penny.

"Why, a piece of it fell on my very own head!" answered Chicken Little.

"I will run with you!" said Henny Penny.

So Chicken Little and Henny Penny ran and ran through the red, orange, yellow, and brown leaves. They ran and ran past the tall oak trees. They ran into Goosey Loosey.

"Chicken Little and Henny Penny, what's wrong?" asked Goosey Loosey.

"The sky is falling, the sky is falling! We must run and warn the king!" cried Chicken Little and Henny Penny.

"How do you know the sky is falling?" asked Goosey Loosey.

"Why, a piece of it fell on my very own head!" answered Chicken Little.

"I will run with you!" said Goosey Loosey.

So Chicken Little, Henny Penny, and Goosey Loosey ran and ran through the red, orange, yellow, and brown leaves. They ran and ran past the tall oak trees. They ran into Turkey Lurkey.

"Chicken Little, Henny Penny, and Goosey Loosey, what's wrong?" asked Turkey Lurkey.

"The sky is falling, the sky is falling! We must run and warn the king!" cried Chicken Little, Henny Penny, and Goosey Loosey.

"How do you know the sky is falling?" asked Turkey Lurkey.

"Why, a piece of it fell on my very own head!" answered Chicken Little.

"I will run with you!" said
Turkey Lurkey.

So Chicken Little, Henny
Penny, Goosey Loosey, and
Turkey Lurkey ran and ran
through the red, orange, yellow,
and brown leaves. They ran
and ran past the tall oak trees.
They ran into Foxy Loxy.

"Chicken Little, Henny Penny, Goosey Loosey, and Turkey Lurkey, what's wrong?" asked Foxy Loxy.

"The sky is falling, the sky is falling! We must run and warn the king!" cried Chicken Little, Henny Penny, Goosey Loosey, and Turkey Lurkey.

"How do you know the sky
is falling?" asked Foxy Loxy.
"Why, a piece of it fell on
my very own head!" answered
Chicken Little.

"You will be safe in my den," said clever Foxy Loxy. "You can hide in there. I will run and warn the king."

"Oh, thank you, thank you!" said Chicken Little, Henny Penny, Goosey Loosey, and Turkey Lurkey.

So Chicken Little, Henny Penny, Goosey Loosey, and Turkey Lurkey followed Foxy Loxy. They followed him through the red, yellow, orange, and brown leaves. They followed him past the tall oak trees. They followed him right into his den. And they were never seen or heard from again.

Have you ever jumped to a conclusion? This means that something happens and you believe whatever first comes to your mind, or the worst possible option, to be true. Like, your portion of dessert is gone and you blame your brother. Or there's mud on the floor and you say your dog did it before really knowing.

Well, Chicken Little jumps to a very imaginative conclusion when an acorn falls on her head: that the sky is falling. She is so upset and concerned that she tells everyone that she sees. And they all go together to warn the king. But before they reach the king, one more animal joins in, the sly, hungry fox. They are tricked into his den, never to come out again.

The story of *Chicken Little* teaches us to think before jumping to conclusions. If Chicken Little had only looked on the ground around her, perhaps she would have seen the acorn that had just hit her and she wouldn't have been so unreasonably afraid. And if her animal friends had thought more about her story, perhaps they could have helped her realize the truth, instead of being tricked into a fox's dinner!

The *Chicken Little* story is very simple, but that's why it's easy to remember. It also uses words that rhyme, or sound alike: Henny Penny, Goosey Loosey, Turkey Lurkey, and Foxy Loxy. If you were to add a character, what would you name it? Doggie Loggie, Ducky Lucky, Bunny Funny, Birdie Lirdie . . .

ABOUT THE AUTHOR

M. J. York has an undergraduate degree in English and history, and a master's degree in library science. M. J. lives in a brick house like the Three Little Pigs and bakes bread like the Little Red Hen.

ABOUT THE ILLUSTRATOR

Teri Weidner grew up in Fairport, New York where she spent much of her free time drawing horses and other animals. Today, she is delighted to have a career illustrating books for children. She lives in Portsmouth, New Hampshire with her husband Chris, their son Nick, and a menagerie of pets.